This Little Tiger
Book Belongs To:

_____

_____

_____

_____

for Kelly, John and Pam
~S.B.
for Di, Alan,
Warne and Eydie
~N.W.

LITTLE TIGER PRESS
1 The Coda Centre, 189 Munster Road, London SW6 6AW
www.littletigerpress.com
This paperback edition published in 2001
First published in Great Britain 2001
Text & Illustrations © 2001 Sam Banfield and Nic Watts
Sam Banfield and Nic Watts have asserted their rights
to be identified as the author and illustrator of this work
under the Copyright, Designs and Patents Act, 1988.
Printed in Belgium
1 3 5 7 9 10 8 6 4 2

Stanley Bones

Sam Banfield and Nic Watts

Little Tiger Press

London

Stanley Bones collected things. Everything that was beautiful or rare was stashed away in a secret place in Stanley's mansion, where he lived with his faithful butler, Montague. He didn't pay for anything he collected. He stole it.

Stanley Bones was the craftiest, most infamous Dog Burglar in town! One day Stanley noticed a big headline in the local paper. "WOW!, Montague," he barked. "THIS IS IT! Our biggest job yet!"

First, they had to work it all out.
"Leave the info to me," said Montague, clicking
away at his super Monti-o-matic computer.
Soon their master plan was ready . . .

Stanley kitted himself
out in his burglar gear,
while Montague packed
the truck with everything
they would need to make
a quick getaway.
"Meet me outside the
Museum at midnight,
Montague." said Stanley,
as he climbed out
through the window.

Stanley's route to the Museum was over the snowy rooftops.

That way, he wouldn't be spotted by the dreaded Inspector Mouse.

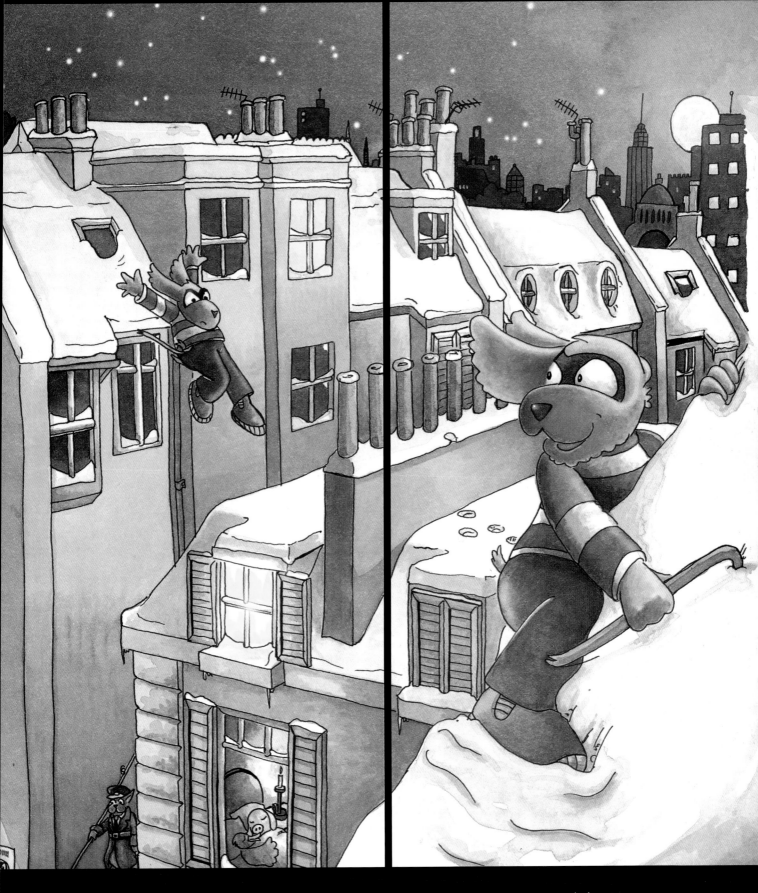

The pesky little creature was always on the lookout . . . . dead set on catching the famous Dog Burglar.

At last Stanley Bones reached the Museum.
The next bit was tricky. He waited on the
roof for the security guards to arrive . . .

then he jumped down on to the top of the moving van!
The van drove through the gates, and Stanley hid in the
snowy yard until the guards were safe inside.
"Brrh, it's as cold as a penguin's nose out here," he shivered.

As soon as the guards had gone, Stanley shinned up the wall, and in through an open window. Was it all clear? No it wasn't! Two security guards were walking towards him!

But Stanley was a master of disguise!
"Dead boring job, this," said one of the guards. "Who'd want to steal a dinosaur, anyway?"

When the coast was clear, Stanley Bones crept towards some double doors and opened them. "Rampaging Rottweilers!" he exclaimed. "They didn't mention these laser beams in the Museum's Guide Book! What shall I do now?"

But Stanley wasn't called the Master Dog Burglar
for nothing! With a dodge here, and a leap there,
he finally reached the last door . . .

"Help!" gasped Stanley. "What a MAMMOTH job!"
He began quickly to dismantle the bones. There was no time
to lose. Montague would be waiting outside for a quick getaway.

The job done, Stanley leapt from the window,
and made his getaway in the waiting truck.

Almost at once, the guards arrived.
"Stone the crows!" one of them shouted.
"Someone's gone and stolen our dinosaur!
Quick! Phone for Inspector Mouse!"

Within minutes, the great Inspector Mouse
was at the scene of the crime.
"Tell everyone to keep their paws off things
till I've had a good sniff around," he ordered.

"Aha," he said.

"Mmm, interesting," he murmured

"So that's where they went,"

"Right lads, after them!"

The snow had left a perfect set of tyre marks,
and soon Inspector Mouse was hot on the trail.
The tyre marks stopped by some double gates.
"Aha, I smell a rat," said Inspector Mouse.
"Or should I say, a bone!"

He was beginning to suspect who
the mysterious dinosaur thief was!
Inspector Mouse and his team burst
through the gates . . .

and followed the tyre marks
to the face of a huge rock.
"So the truck went through
solid rock," he said.
"Impossible!" But it took
only a few seconds for the
brilliant Inspector to spot
a cunning device at the base
of a nearby statue - a lever!

"The clever dog!" growled the Inspector. "But not clever enough!" Two of the Inspector's Cat Police pulled the levers, and C - R - E - A - K the rock face swung open.

"Aha, I thought as much!" said the Inspector. "Stanley Bones, we meet at last!"

It was useless for Stanley to try to hide his hoard of treasures.
"OK, Inspector," he sighed. "You've collared me at last!"
"A BIG sentence for a BIG crime," declared the Inspector.

"We won't see Stanley Bones and his mouldy mole around for many years to come."
"Don't be too sure of that," muttered Stanley . . .

More books to treasure from
Little Tiger Press

Who's that scratching at my door?

Wait for me, Little Tiger!

Fireman PiggyWiggy

The Very Noisy Night

Titus's Troublesome Tooth

Little Bear's Grandad

Little Mouse and the Big Red Apple

For information regarding any of the above titles or for our catalogue,
please contact us: Little Tiger Press, 1 The Coda Centre, 189 Munster Road,
London SW6 6AW, UK
Telephone: 020 7385 6333 Fax: 020 7385 7333 e-mail: info@littletiger.co.uk
www.littletigerpress.com